He Loves Me!
He Truly Loves Me!

The Story of Mupsie and Me
and How We Came To Be!

Devon Michael
Sangiovanni

Balboa Press books may be ordered through booksellers or by contacting:

Balboa Press
A Division of Hay House
1663 Liberty Drive
Bloomington, IN 47403
www.balboapress.com
844-682-1282

For hardcover copies and all Mupsie merchandise
please visit us at our website at
www.mupsie.com

All Illustrations in this book are hand painted watercolors by Joanna D. Sacksteder. No illustrations may be reproduced in any way. The views expressed in this work are solely those of the author and do not necessarily reflect the views of the publisher, and the publisher hereby disclaims any responsibility for them.

Because of the dynamic nature of the Internet, any web addresses or links contained in this book may have changed since publication and may no longer be valid. The views expressed in this work are solely those of the author and do not necessarily reflect the views of the publisher, and the publisher hereby disclaims any responsibility for them.

ISBN: 978-1-9822-3606-9 (sc)
ISBN: 978-1-9822-3607-6 (e)

Library of Congress Control Number: 2019915342

Printed in the United States of America.

Balboa Press rev. date: 03/11/2021

BALBOA.PRESS
A DIVISION OF HAY HOUSE

Coming Soon!

I Love Him!
I Truly Love Him!

She Loves Me!
She Truly Loves Me!

Mupsie Goes to Hollywood!

Forever in My Heart

Preface

To all parents-

It is in the presence of love that all children can grow and prosper. As parents it is our responsibility to provide them with that love. We owe it to this little child a sense of security, that he or she is well taken care of and that they may feel loved and understood in all situations. Encourage your child's strengths and help them with their weaknesses, it is in this experience of you that they will find their own strength to grow and prosper. It is to this end that I bring you The Mupsie Series.

Godspeed-
Devon Michael Sangiovanni

He Loves Me!
He Truly Loves Me!

To Mups…
  the Love of my life…

It all started a long, long time ago
   with a tiny, little furball kitten with
      big, beautiful blue eyes and
         a heart to match!

He was happy to be alive
   and full of awe and wonder!
      His fur was *so* soft and cuddly,
         and his heart was full of love!

He was born with a few
adorable little sisters...

And every day he would sit by the phone
and wait for it to ring...

All excited to see
who the *lucky* one would be
who would get to share all
this love with me!!!

And every day
he would sit by the phone
and wait for it to ring...

And every day he would hear John
say the very same thing...
"Yes we have little girl kittens!
What time will you be here?
Okay, see you then!"

And one by one the people would come
and pick up the little girl kittens,
and he would be left behind...
Sad,
so sad...

"But doesn't *any*body want a boy kitten?"
he would sob...he began to think
no one would ever love him!

And he waited...
and he waited,
and he waited,
and he waited...

Day in and day out he would sit by the phone,
and wait for it to ring...
in hopes it would be *someone*,
anyone, who would call for a
little boy kitten...

1 day, 2 days, 3 days, 4...
and the days turned into weeks,
and the weeks turned into months.
Sad,
so sad...

He got sadder and sadder
and mopier and mopier,
he wouldn't even come out of
his cubby to play...

But then one day...

he decided to pray!

He started to feel hope!
He started to feel alive again!
And his little heart,
that was once so big and full of love,
began to grow bigger and bigger
and happier and happier...
and full of love like it used to be!

That night,
   when he fell asleep,
    he had a dream...
     He had a dream about a
      man who was gentle and kind,
       who would call for a little girl kitten,
      but when he came
       he would change his mind!
      Happy!
       Happy, Happy, Happy!

He couldn't *wait* to fall asleep again!
And every night, before he went to bed,
he would pray that the man who was
gentle and kind, would call for a little
girl kitten, but when he came
he would change his mind!

As he dozed off to sleep,
and the good feelings would start to come,
he had a smile on his little face,
as he lulled himself to sleep...
Happy!
Happy,
Happy,
Happy!

The next day when he woke up,
he raced down to the phone and
waited for it to ring!

But, when he heard the phone ring,
he heard *John* say the very same thing?!
"Yes we have little girl kittens!
What time will you be here?!
Okay, see you then!"

RING! RING!

But this time,

this time it was different...

He *believed* that the man who was gentle and kind,

would call for a little girl kitten,

but when he came he would change his mind!

And he prayed...

and he prayed,

and he prayed,

and he prayed...

DING! DONG!

...the doorbell rang!
When the man walked in he *knew* it was him,
the man was gentle and kind!

As they walked toward the kitchen,
  John handed him the kittens,
    but when he sat down in the chair,
      he had a look of despair...

I didn't know what he was thinking,
could it be he had an inkling?!

It was then that he turned and
he saw me sitting there!

Our hearts began to flutter,
and love filled the air...
could it *be* he was the one
who was the answer to my prayers?

He knelt right down beside me,
 and put me in his arms,
  I knew right then and there,
   that I was safe from harm...

I closed my big blue eyes
 and I began to purr,
  he tickled my little belly
   and my soft and cuddly fur...

I knew right from the start,
that we would never be apart,
we would always be together...
Forever in my Heart!

"He Loves Me!
He Truly Loves Me!"

"Put your coat on,
we're going home!"